Common Sense

PRAISE FOR *STORYSHARES*

"One of the brightest innovators and game-changers in the education industry."
– Forbes

"Your success in applying research-validated practices to promote literacy serves as a valuable model for other organizations seeking to create evidence-based literacy programs."

- Library of Congress

"We need powerful social and educational innovation, and Storyshares is breaking new ground. The organization addresses critical problems facing our students and teachers. I am excited about the strategies it brings to the collective work of making sure every student has an equal chance in life."
– Teach For America

"Around the world, this is one of the up-and-coming trailblazers changing the landscape of literacy and education."
- International Literacy Association

"It's the perfect idea. There's really nothing like this. I mean wow, this will be a wonderful experience for young people."   - Andrea Davis Pinkney, Executive Director, Scholastic

"Reading for meaning opens opportunities for a lifetime of learning. Providing emerging readers with engaging texts that are designed to offer both challenges and support for each individual will improve their lives for years to come. Storyshares is a wonderful start."
- David Rose, Co-founder of CAST & UDL

Common Sense

Jamie Todd

STORYSHARES

Story Share, Inc.
New York. Boston. Philadelphia.

Storyshares
Story Share, Inc.
24 N. Bryn Mawr Avenue #340
Bryn Mawr, PA 19010-3304
www.storyshares.org

Inspiring reading with a new kind of book.

Interest Level: High School
Grade Level Equivalent: 4.1

9781642611427

Book design by Storyshares

Printed in the United States of America

Storyshares Presents

1

Dr. Berg dropped a stack of papers on his desk. Dawson, Valentina, Perry, Gael, and Marina flinched in their chairs. After a moment, Dr. Berg looked at the five of them.

"Do you know what these are?" Dr. Berg asked.

None of them said anything.

"Well?"

"A stack of papers?" Gael said, twisting her orange hair.

"Yes . . . but I was looking for a more specific answer, Miss Wilde," Dr. Berg said, clenching his teeth.

Gael looked at the others. Her friends didn't offer any information. She looked back at the principal and shrugged.

"Very well. Be aware that none of you are leaving my office until you explain your actions."

"You can't keep us out of class!" Valentina exclaimed, looking back and forth between her friends for confirmation, her blue hair swishing.

"Oh but I can. And if none of you fess up within the next couple of minutes, I will be calling all of your parents too, Miss Robin." Dr. Berg leaned back in his hair, crossed his arms, and stared at her.

"My parents would support what we did. Isn't that right, Perry?" Valentina looked at her older brother.

"Stand down, little sis," Perry mumbled, running his hand through his blue hair.

"Perry!" Marina exclaimed. "Why would you tell her to stand down after all we accomplished?"

Perry didn't answer. He glanced at Valentina, who looked at him in disbelief. Perry looked at his lap in shame.

"Well, if we fight our punishment, then he'll make it worse. Val, you know how our parents would react if they got a phone call," Perry said.

"They would be proud of us," Valentina growled.

Perry didn't answer.

"Well," Dawson said, pulling out a comb to attend to his pink hair. "Looks like we're at a stand-still then."

Dr. Berg narrowed his eyes. "I doubt Miss Wilde and Mr. Robin would like to have this on their permanent record of their senior year. Mr. Blyden and Miss Stevens can't afford it either, as you two are in your junior year— the year colleges look at the most. Miss Robin could get away with it, as she's only a sophomore, but the severity of it still wouldn't look good."

Perry snapped his head up. "How dare you threaten us like that," he spat. "We were fighting for our right to create a club that is inclusive."

"You're not even one of them," Dr. Berg said, leaning toward the five friends.

"No, but my sister is. And I will fight like hell for her to have more rights, even on the small scale of this school. You have no right to oppress my sister and my friends."

"Mr. Robin, if you do not wish to be expelled, you will not open your mouth from this moment on unless I directly ask you a question. Do you understand?"

Perry's body shook in anger. His eyes flicked back and forth between the principal's eyes. His upper lip twitched. "Understood."

Gael gently pulled on Perry's shoulder, forcing him to lean back. Perry didn't resist, but his anger didn't cease.

"Now then, for the four of you, who I will still allow a chance to explain yourselves . . . What is the meaning of the pamphlets?" Dr. Berg asked Dawson, Gael, Marina, and Valentina.

The four of them glanced at each other, silently asking who should explain or if they even should explain.

Dr. Berg huffed. "Okay. Fine. How about I make this easy for you? Miss Wilde, you are the eldest of those allowed to speak. Why don't you explain?" Dr. Berg said.

Gael fixed her sunglasses and smiled. "It would be my pleasure."

2

"It was Dawson's idea," Gael began, "but the rest of us were quick to support it. Being the history buff, it was my thought as to how we would go about it, but the original concept was Dawson's. It took us, mmm . . . I'd say two or three days to write and finalize the pamphlet. I'm happy with it," she said.

"Thank you, Miss Wilde, but I want to know about the reason behind what the five of you did," Dr. Berg said.

"I'll get there, sir." Gael gathered her hair together and began braiding it. "I guess I should begin by explaining our sexualities." She looked around at her friends. They each nodded. "Dawson is gay, Valentina is bisexual, I'm demisexual, Perry is straight, and Marina is a lesbian. We—"

"Demisexual? You made up that word. I've never heard of that before. Why would you make up such a thing?" Dr. Berg asked.

Gael cocked her head, and her expression hardened. "Sir, I did not make up that word. It is a real word, thank you very much. Demisexuality is defined as—"

"And why would someone who is straight want to be a part of this?"

"Perry supports his sister and his friends. That's why it's called a Gay-Straight Alli—"

"None of this makes sense."

"IT WOULD MAKE SENSE IF YOU LET ME FINISH!" Gael snapped, finally growing impatient.

"Do NOT raise your voice at me, Miss Wilde, or you will suffer the same consequences as Mr. Robin," Mr. Berg said, slamming his hands on his desk and standing.

She looked up at him. "It would be a better consequence than suffering this injustice."

Dr. Berg seethed. "MISS Wilde, please remove yourself from this room. I will deal with you separately after."

"And if I refuse?"

Dr. Berg narrowed his eyes at Gael. "I will call your parents and kick you out of your student government position."

"Do it. I dare you."

"I will. After I get a straight answer as to why you five did this. Now GET OUT OF MY OFFICE!"

Gael stood, flipped him off, and walked out of his office.

3

"Miss Stevens," Dr. Berg said, turning to Marina. "Please continue where Miss Wilde left off."

She glanced at Valentina, Dawson, and Perry.

Perry nodded.

"It's okay, Marina," Dawson said. "Go on. If you forget anything, I'll help you."

She looked in Dr. Berg's direction but not directly at him. "I will start off where Gael was speaking before you so rudely interrupted her."

Dr. Berg opened his mouth to speak, but Marina kept talking. "Demisexuality is defined as not having sexual attraction unless a deep emotional connection is established between two individuals. Gael is demisexual. As far as I am aware, she's known for about a year. I have known I am attracted to girls since I was in eighth grade. Dawson . . . ?"

"I have known I was gay since I was in seventh grade," Dawson said.

Marina looked at Valentina.

"I have known I was bisexual since last year, since ninth grade," Valentina said, putting her shoulder-length blue hair in a ponytail.

"About a month ago, Dawson came up with the idea of creating a Gay-Straight Alliance club since our school doesn't have one. We all know other people that are gay, lesbian, bi, demi, grey, ace, pan, etc." Marina said.

"Making up more words, are we?" Dr. Berg said, crossing his arms again.

"If you want, you can look up every word we've said. You will see how real they are. Please let me continue, or you will never hear the reasons behind our actions."

Dr. Berg didn't respond.

"Now, it was Dawson's idea, as Gael said, but she figured out how we would go about getting the idea out to the student body to get support. Even though we only need two people to create a club, and there are five of us, we wanted others to know about it.

"Gael loves history. She suggested that we model our advertisement after the pamphlet by Thomas Paine, 'Common Sense.' That's the pamphlet that advocated for the colonists to fight for their independence against Britain.

"See, with the exception of Perry and usually Valentina, we are considered very weird among our peers. So we distributed the advertisements anonymously in hopes that we would get support from those who might not support us otherwise. Then, after about a week, we made new posters that included our names."

"Marina, I would like to take it from here, if I may," Dawson said.

"Of course."

"So, besides the fact that the majority of us aren't straight, we're also weird among our peers for other reasons. I am a gay African American with pink hair. I am president of the fashion club. Valentina is bi with shoulder length, curly blue hair. She is Puerto Rican, and she isn't goth, but she is definitely headed in that direction. Gael is from France, has long orange hair, wears wild clothes, is demisexual, and is treasurer for the senior class.

"Perry is straight. He has blue hair that is considered long for a guy, is the guitarist for a band, is Puerto Rican but doesn't look it, and is very protective of his little sister. Marina is the palest person I know, and her maroon hair is cut in a pixie style. She has three piercings in her left ear, is a lesbian, and plays bass in the band with Perry.

"There's nothing wrong with any of us. But because of our 'differences,' we're considered tangents," Dawson explained. "Our peers think we are weird. I say we're unique. We have personality. We are a minority, some of us more than others, but we all deserve to have a club where we can feel safe and comfortable. You are the only thing in our way.

"That is why, sir, we made the pamphlets. And whether or not you acknowledge our club as an official school club here, the club will be created. All six of us will attend and, assuming our pamphlets did as well as we expected, so will more of the student body."

Dawson looked Dr. Berg straight in the eye, challenging him to say something derogatory. After a moment, Dr. Berg looked at the others, then back at Dawson. "Mr. Blyden, while you made a good speech just now, I still forbid you and your friends from—" he began, but Marina cut him off.

"You're a homophobe!" Marina half yelled, half spat. "The state's court of appeals ruled that we, the students, are allowed to create a Gay-Straight Alliance club."

Dr. Berg's face paled slightly. "Miss Stevens, I—"

"And if you continue to refuse us the right to create a Gay-Straight Alliance club, to make an official club of the school, we will not hesitate in taking you to court over this," Marina continued.

Dr. Berg blinked in surprise. "MISS Stevens, is that a threat?"

Marina leaned forward and whispered, "Yes, and you would lose."

Dr. Berg started to squirm in his chair. He looked between the group of them. He cleared his throat. "Miss Robin, go get Miss Wilde from out in the hall," he told her.

Valentina looked at Dawson, Perry, and Marina, then got up and walked into the hall. Marina continued to stare at Dr. Berg, causing him to squirm more in his seat. After a moment, Valentina and Gael walked back in to Dr. Berg's office and sat back down in their chairs.

"Miss Wilde, Miss Stevens, Miss Robin, Mr. Robin, and Mr. Blyden . . . After . . . careful consideration, I have decided to let you all have your gay club and—"

"Gay-Straight Alliance," Marina and Gael said together.

"Yes, that. I have decided you may have your club, and it will be an official school club, so long as you don't cause me any trouble."

"We'll try not to," Gael said, "but 'trouble' is my middle name."

"And my nickname," Marina said, finally leaning away from the principal.

"Right. Now, all of you get out of my office."

Perry, Gael, Dawson, Marina, and Valentina walked out of Dr. Berg's office glowing with pride. Perry glanced at Gael, and when she caught him, she blushed slightly and looked down. Dawson and Valentina talked about fashion. Marina held back, waiting outside Dr. Berg's office. Valentina turned to ask Marina something. Upon seeing her still at the principal's door, she called to her.

"I'll be there in a minute," Marina said. She turned to look back inside the office. "I have something to do first." Marina walked back inside toward Dr. Berg's desk.

"Now what?" he asked.

"I'll be needing those back," Marina said, nodding to the pile of pamphlets still in the center of the desk.

Dr. Berg waved his hand. "Fine, take them. Then get out of my hair."

"Gladly." Marina took the pile and walked out. She walked all the way back to her locker, unlocked it, and put the pile inside, every pamphlet except one. She grabbed the one on top and examined it.

Some schools regard students as being one and the same. They leave little or no distinction between them, whereas, in truth, they are not only different but have different sexualities. Clubs such as this one are produced by both wants and by necessity. One encourages a sense of community; the other creates distinctions.

Join Perry Robin, Gael Wilde, Dawson Blyden, Marina Stevens, and Valentina Robin in their fight for the creation of a Gay-Straight Alliance club. Everyone deserves a place to feel welcome and safe. It's common sense.

About The Author

Jamie Todd is a contributing author to the Storyshares library.

About The Publisher

Story Shares is a nonprofit focused on supporting the millions of teens and adults who struggle with reading by creating a new shelf in the library specifically for them. The ever-growing collection features content that is compelling and culturally relevant for teens and adults, yet still readable at a range of lower reading levels.

Story Shares generates content by engaging deeply with writers, bringing together a community to create this new kind of book. With more intriguing and approachable stories to choose from, the teens and adults who have fallen behind are improving their skills and beginning to discover the joy of reading. For more information, visit storyshares.org.

Easy to Read. Hard to Put Down.

www.ingramcontent.com/pod-product-compliance
Lightning Source LLC
Chambersburg PA
CBHW071231170626
46809CB00005BA/2026